by

Lindsay Cibos
and
Jared Hodges

HAMBURG // LONDON // LOS ANGELES // TOKYO

**visit us at www.abdopublishing.com**

Reinforced library bound edition published in 2009 by Spotlight, a division of ABDO Publishing Group, 8000 West 78th Street, Edina, Minnesota 55439. This edition reprinted by arrangement with TOKYOPOP Inc. www.tokyopop.com



| | |
|---|---|
| Production Artist | James Dashiell |
| Cover Design | Raymond Makowski |
| Editor | Jodi Bryson |
| Digital Imaging Manager | Chris Buford |

**Library of Congress Cataloging-in-Publication Data**

Cibos, Lindsay.
Peach Fuzz / by Lindsay Cibos and Jared Hodges.
v. cm.
Summary: When Amanda begs her parents for a pet and they relent and get her a ferret, the previously calm household turns chaotic, and even worse, the ferret learns to fear Amanda, who knows nothing about how to take care of a pet.
Contents: Vol. 1. Peach Fuzz -- Vol. 2. Show & tell -- Vol. 3. Prince Edwin.
ISBN 978-1-59961-571-4 (vol. 1: Peach Fuzz)
1. Graphic novels. [1. Graphic novels. 2. Ferrets as pets--Fiction. 3. Pets--Fiction.] I. Hodges, Jared. II. Title.
PZ7.7.C53Pe 2008
[Fic]--dc22
2008002197



Spotlight

All Spotlight books have reinforced library binding and are manufactured in the United States of America.

# Table of Contents

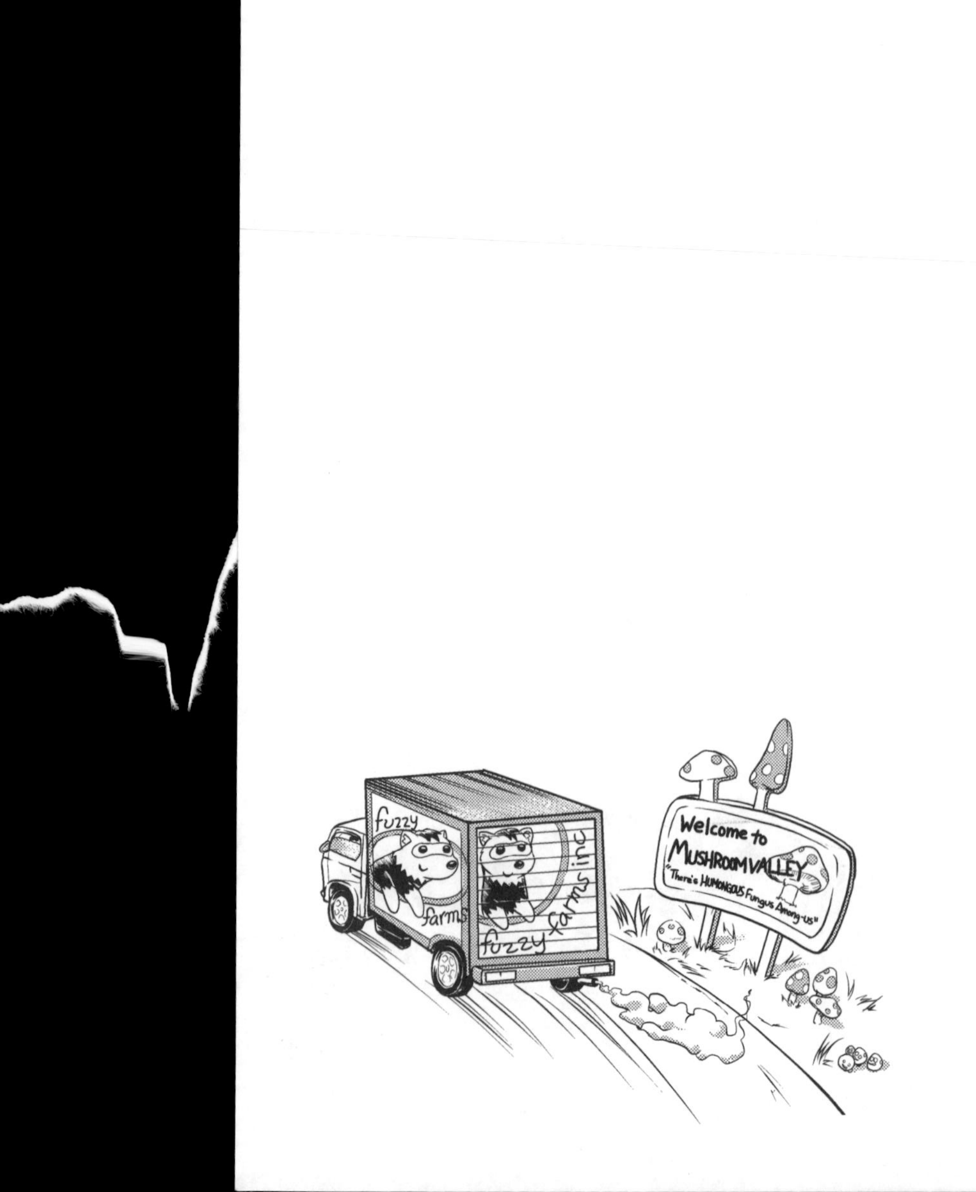
fuzzy farms
fuzzy farms inc
Welcome to
MUSHROOM VALLEY
"There's HUMONGOUS Fungus Among-us"

Press

Fwump

dogs reptiles Fish Ferrets &More!
SUPER!PETS
PARROT SALE!
WE CARE
SLAM!

AMANDA...
Dash

SUPER!PETS
EXOTIC VARIETIES
PET SUPPLIES!
SP GUARANTEE!
A PET IS A BIG RESPONSIBILITY.
YOU HAVE TO FEED IT, CLEA--
Ding-a-ling...
--I KNOOOOW, MOM!
SUPER!PETS
WE CARE

Chapter 1
First encounter
ENGLISH
ENGLISH 4

COLORKids!
62
62
PACK

NAME: AMANDA KELLER
AGE: 9 YEARS OLD
AFTER MONTHS AND MONTHS OF BEGGING, PLEADING, AND BARGAINING, AMANDA'S MOTHER FINALLY AGREED TO LET HER GET A PET.
SHE CAREFULLY EXAMINED ALL OF THE PET SHOP'S ANIMALS... BUT...
ANIMALS EVERYWHERE!! ♡
...
fish food
DOG
MOUSE
CAT
HAMSTER
fish
NONE OF THEM CAUGHT HER INTEREST. THEY DIDN'T HAVE THAT SPECIAL SOMETHING.
THEY WERE ALL SO BORING.
EVERYONE HAS THESE.
BUT THEN, SHE SAW THE FERRETS.
diagram of a ferret
burglar's mask
"s-curve" back
long slender tail
button nose
shark mouth
digging claws
tube-shaped body
paddle feet

THEY WERE SO FUN WHEN THEY PLAYED.
WICK!
AND THEY USED THE LITTER BOX!
GRRRR!
THEY WERE SO SWEET WHEN THEY SLEPT.
OOOH! CLAW TO THE NOSE!!
THE PERFECT EXOTIC PET.
CUTE!
WOW!
KIM, AGE 10 (AMANDA'S FRIEND)
MIMI, AGE 9 (AMANDA'S FRIEND)
BUNNY
MOMMY, I FOUND WHAT I WANT!
LET'S GET A FERRET!
AMANDA
QUEEN OF THE FERRETS

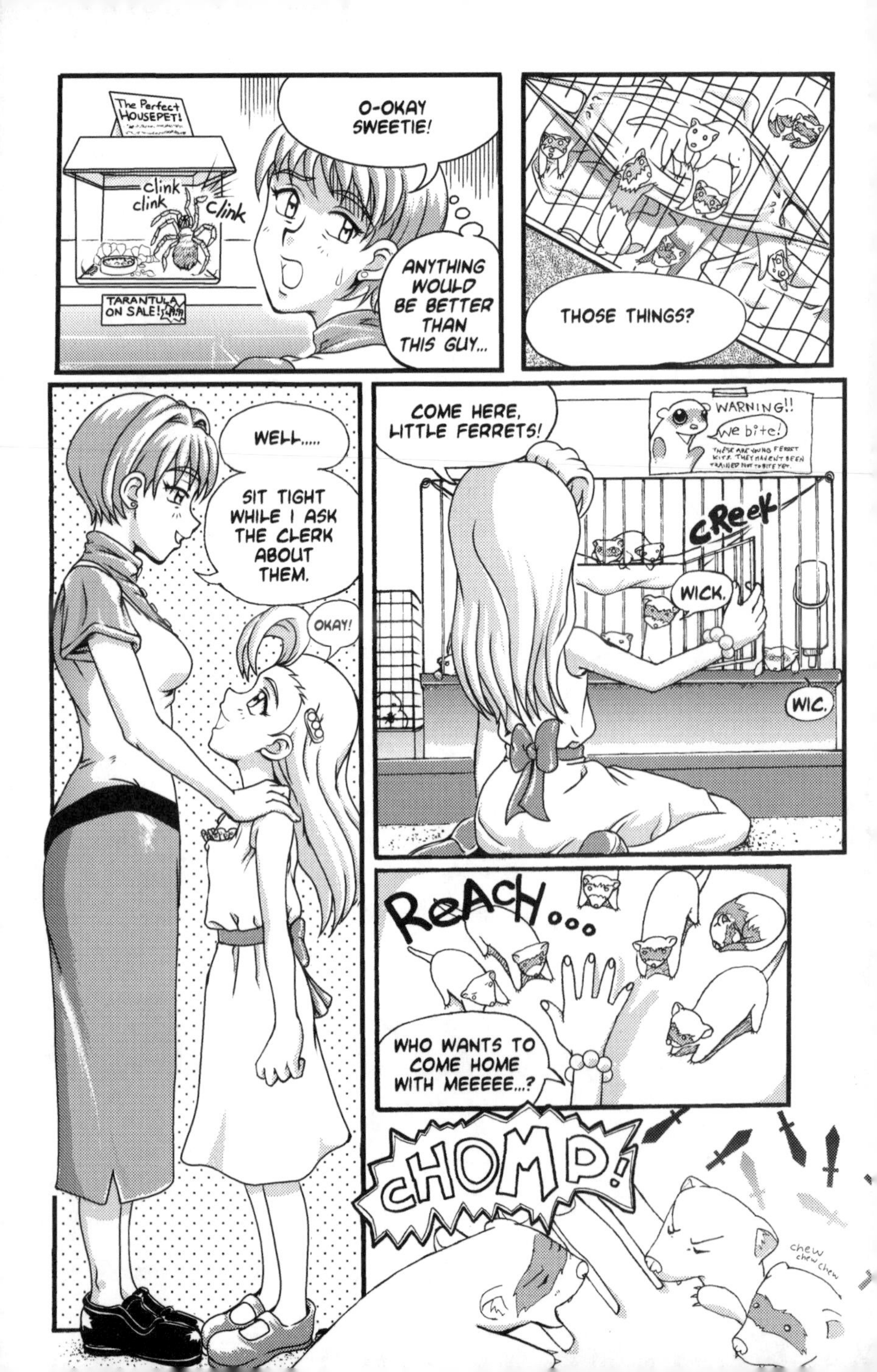

The Perfect HOUSEPET!
clink
clink
clink
TARANTULA ON SALE!
O-OKAY SWEETIE!
ANYTHING WOULD BE BETTER THAN THIS GUY...
THOSE THINGS?
WELL.....
SIT TIGHT WHILE I ASK THE CLERK ABOUT THEM.
OKAY!
COME HERE, LITTLE FERRETS!
WARNING!!
we bite!
THESE ARE YOUNG FERRET KITS. THEY HAVEN'T BEEN TRAINED NOT TO BITE YET.
CReek
WICK.
WIC.
ReACH...
WHO WANTS TO COME HOME WITH MEEEEE...?
CHOMP!
chew chew chew

OW!
THROB THROB
MAYBE I SHOULD GET A HAMSTER INSTEAD...
NO!
I ALREADY MADE UP MY MIND TO GET A FERRET!
I JUST NEED TO PICK ONE THAT ISN'T MEAN.
GLARE
HELLO, THERE!
BITE!
ARGH!
ARE YOU ALL LIKE THAT?!
OH!
THAT ONE LOOKS FRIENDLY!
WICK.
WIC.
scratch scratch

POKE
POKE
POKE
?
FLINCH
...EH?!
ZZZ
IT...
IT DIDN'T BITE ME! IT JUST WENT RIGHT BACK TO SLEEP!
PERFECT!
ZZZZZZ
AMANDA...
MOMMY! I FOUND THE ONE I WANT!
IT'S SO PRETTY AND SWEET...
TAP

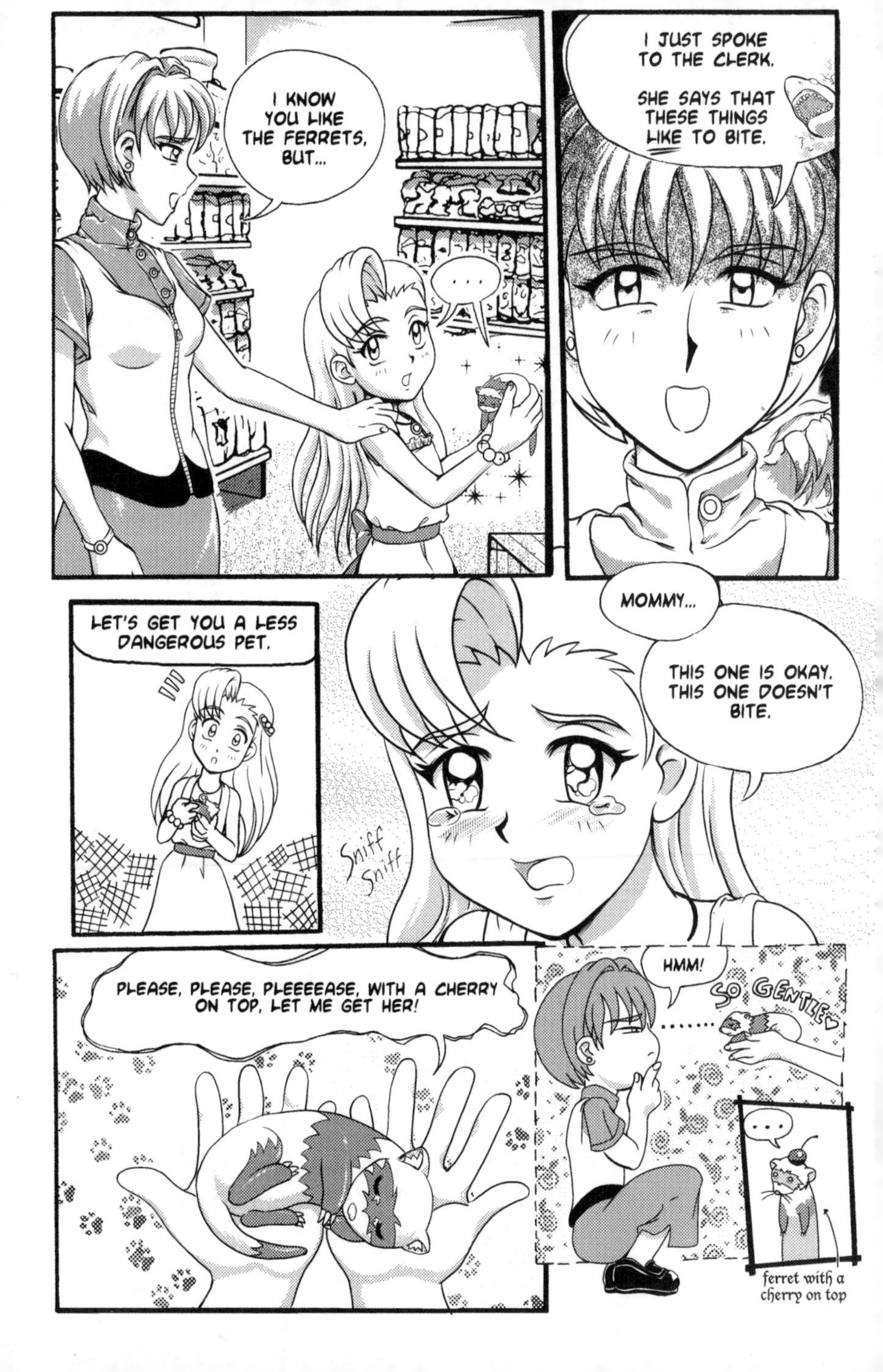
I KNOW YOU LIKE THE FERRETS, BUT...
...
I JUST SPOKE TO THE CLERK.
SHE SAYS THAT THESE THINGS LIKE TO BITE.
LET'S GET YOU A LESS DANGEROUS PET.
MOMMY...
THIS ONE IS OKAY. THIS ONE DOESN'T BITE.
Sniff Sniff
PLEASE, PLEASE, PLEEEEASE, WITH A CHERRY ON TOP, LET ME GET HER!
HMM!
SO GENTLE
...
ferret with a cherry on top

WELL, IT LOOKS HARMLESS ENOUGH...
~whimper~
BUT...
IF IT BITES YOU, WE'RE TAKING IT BACK AND GETTING YOU A SAFER ANIMAL...
LIKE A FISH.
Bloop Bloop
SPLASH
A... FISH?!
BUT, FISH DON'T DO ANYTHING, AND YOU CAN'T PET THEM!
SHOULD WE GIVE THE FERRET A TRIAL RUN?
~ SO ENTHUSIASTIC! ♡
Victory
DON'T WORRY, MOMMY! SHE'D NEVER HURT ME!
CHA-CHING!
IMPROPER FERRET HOLDING TECHNIQUE!!

...Peek
SHE'S SO CUTE! ♡
SUPER! PETS
ZZZ
VROOSH!
WHAT ARE YOU GOING TO CALL HER?
HMM...
A NAME IS A VERY IMPORTANT THING.
WHAT SHOULD I CALL THE FERRET?
I HAVE TO THINK ABOUT IT!
RATTLE RATTLE
SUPER! PETS

YAWNNN!
THUMP!
THUMP!
STRETCH!!
???
??
huh?!
how curious for a wall to interrupt my stretching...
!
THUMP.

LOOK, MOMMY, SHE'S AWAKE!
WICK!!
bump
bump
Fwap
fwump
where am i? what's going on?!
Rumble
Rumble

it's so dark in here!
i can't find an exit!

where are you, my royal subjects?
i must collect my thoughts...
the last thing i remember...

Ferretland
it was a typical day in my kingdom.
parakeet feather
hi!
creek
rumble
kibble
WADOOM
SCREECH x5!
glance
!
slither
Sniff
Sniff
Sniff

ROARRRR
SNORT!
someone help us!!!
HiSsSss
faint
SNATCH
HEE HEE.

i observed the commotion from a safe distance.
. . .
the monsters known to us as handra...
...typical.
princess!
FWITTER
trouble in the courtyard!
FWITTER
yes... i know.
huff huff
requesting permission to call upon the kibble knights for assistance.
bow
of course! it's their duty to protect me.
princess, the knights have never failed at warding off intruders...
...but you should still hide...
...just as a precaution.

fight bravely! do not hesitate to sacrifice yourselves for me.
Kibble Knights... Charge!
. . .
Shh, it's Okay my guinea-steed!
Uwieeee ee
for Kibble...
...and justice!!
Uwieeeeeeee

AWOOOOOOOOOO
the five-headed handra had already attacked us on several occasions this week.
...
gulp...
uwiellle
attack!!
Poke
?!

Shrieekk
yay!
Victory!
it's retreating!
OWWWW...
LEGGO!
Won't let go!
UFGH...
HISS!!
SNAP.
a single blow from a kibble knight's sword usually sent a handra recoiling away in terror. but this one was much more persistent.
!
no! the princess!
fwump!

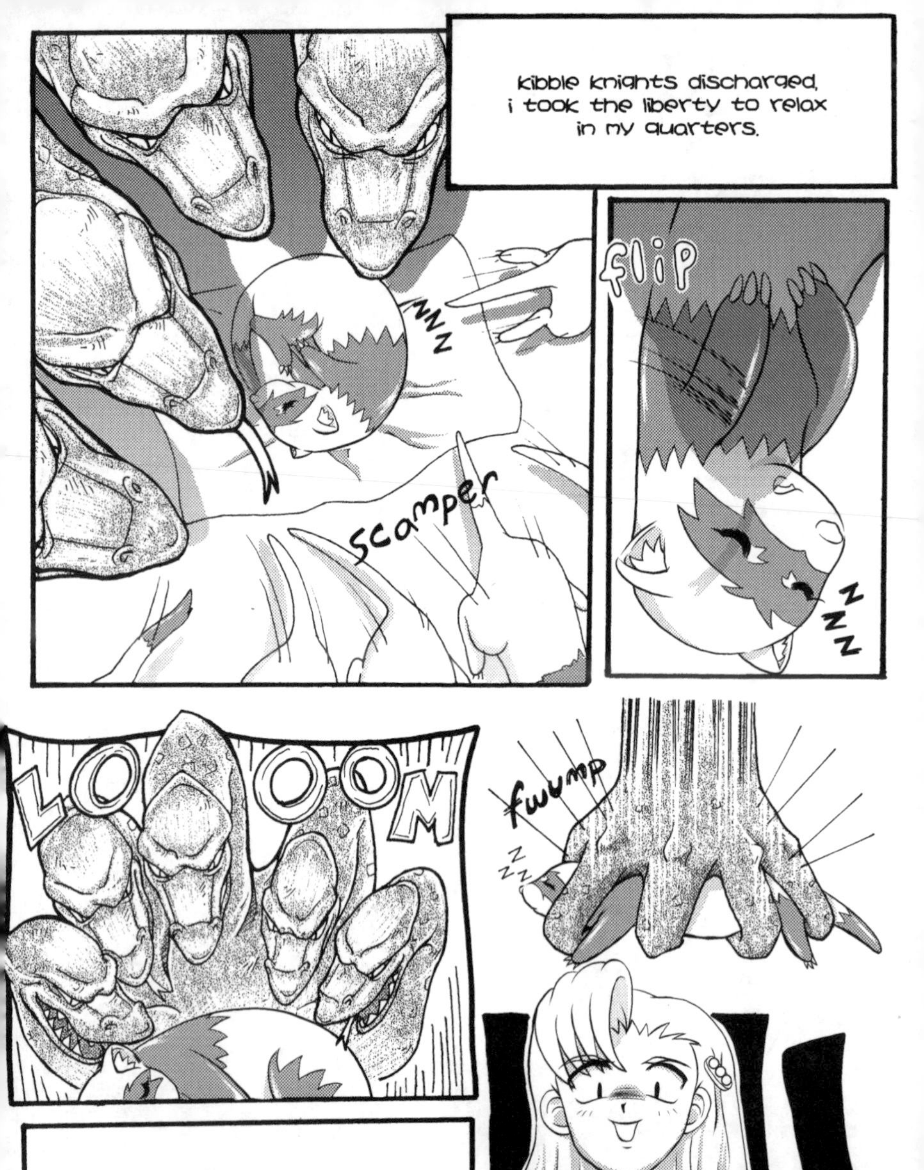
kibble knights discharged, i took the liberty to relax in my quarters.
scamper
flip
LOOOOM
fwump
it was warm, dark, and comfortable.
it wasn't long before i fell into a deep slumber.
PERFECT.

kibble knights, you've failed me. i'll never forgive you!
oh noooooo! the handra must have caught me!
HISSSSs
the only one i can rely on is myself!
FWSK
Scratch scratch scratch
Scratch
WOW, SHE'S SO ACTIVE IN THERE!
SUPER!PETS
scratch scratch
SUPER!PETS
HI!
POP!
SUPER
fling
SUPER!PETS

oh nooo o
WAIT!
leap
FWUMP
WAIT!
ERRTT!
ZAM
AMANDA! DON'T SCREAM! ARE YOU TRYING TO GET ME INTO AN ACCIDENT?!
EH?
Scamper
WHAT WAS THAT!?
SCREECH
FAMICAR

MY FERRET... IT'S GONE!
MOMMY HELP!
IT'S STILL IN THE CAR! CATCH IT, AMANDA!!
BUT...
I DON'T KNOW WHERE SHE WENT!
the royal litter box...
where is it?!
JUST LOOK FOR HER!
AROOOOOo
not again!!

THERE YOU ARE!
WIC!

DON'T LET HER GO AGAIN. I NEED TO FOCUS ON THE ROAD.

Struggle

CALM DOWN, BABY FERRET.
pat pat
fwump
IRK
no more!

YOU CALMER, NOW?
!
oh no!
it's coming back!

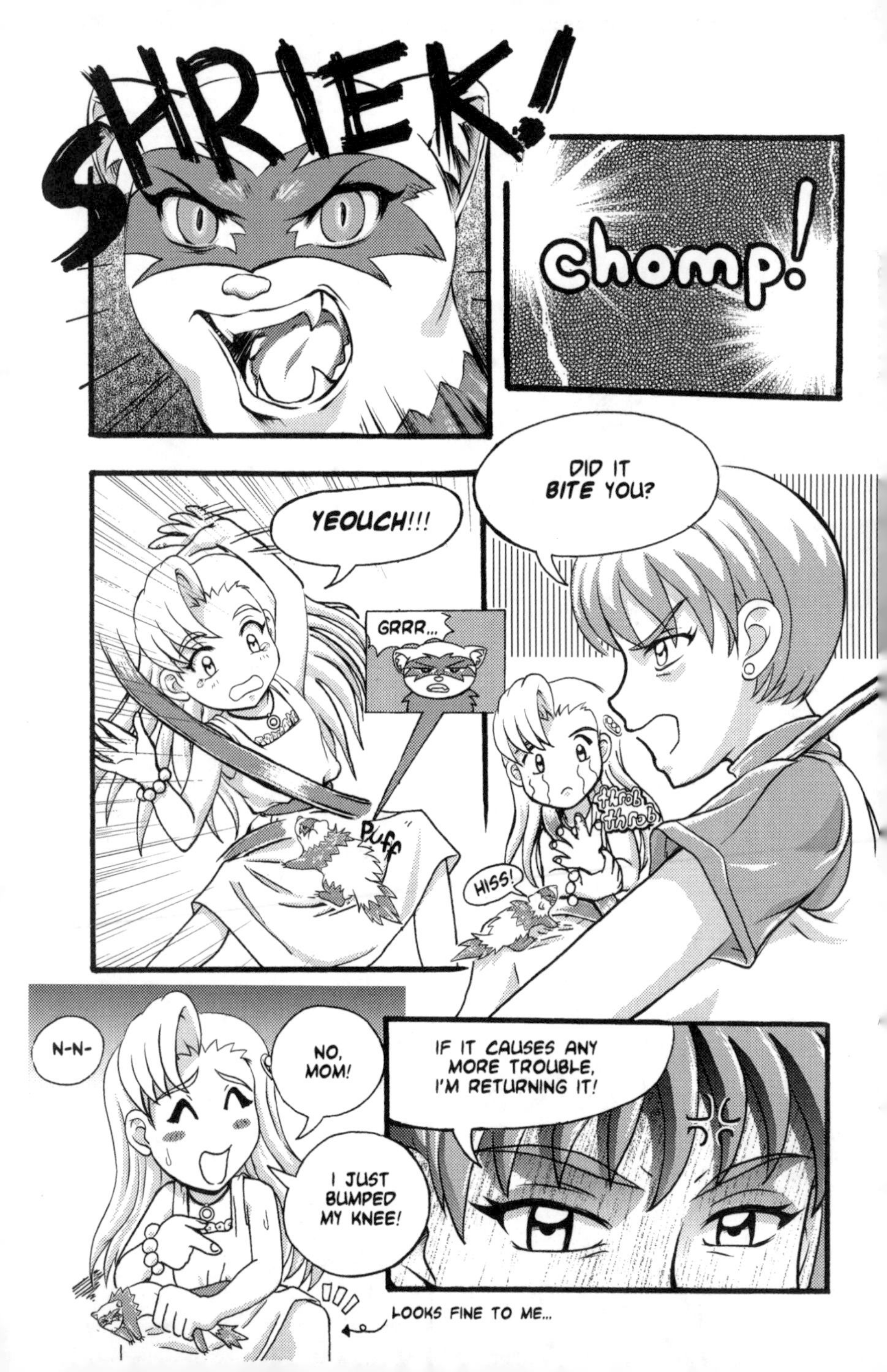
SHRIEK!
chomp!
YEOUCH!!!
DID IT BITE YOU?
GRRR...
Puff
throb throb
HISS!
N-N-
NO, MOM!
I JUST BUMPED MY KNEE!
IF IT CAUSES ANY MORE TROUBLE, I'M RETURNING IT!
LOOKS FINE TO ME...

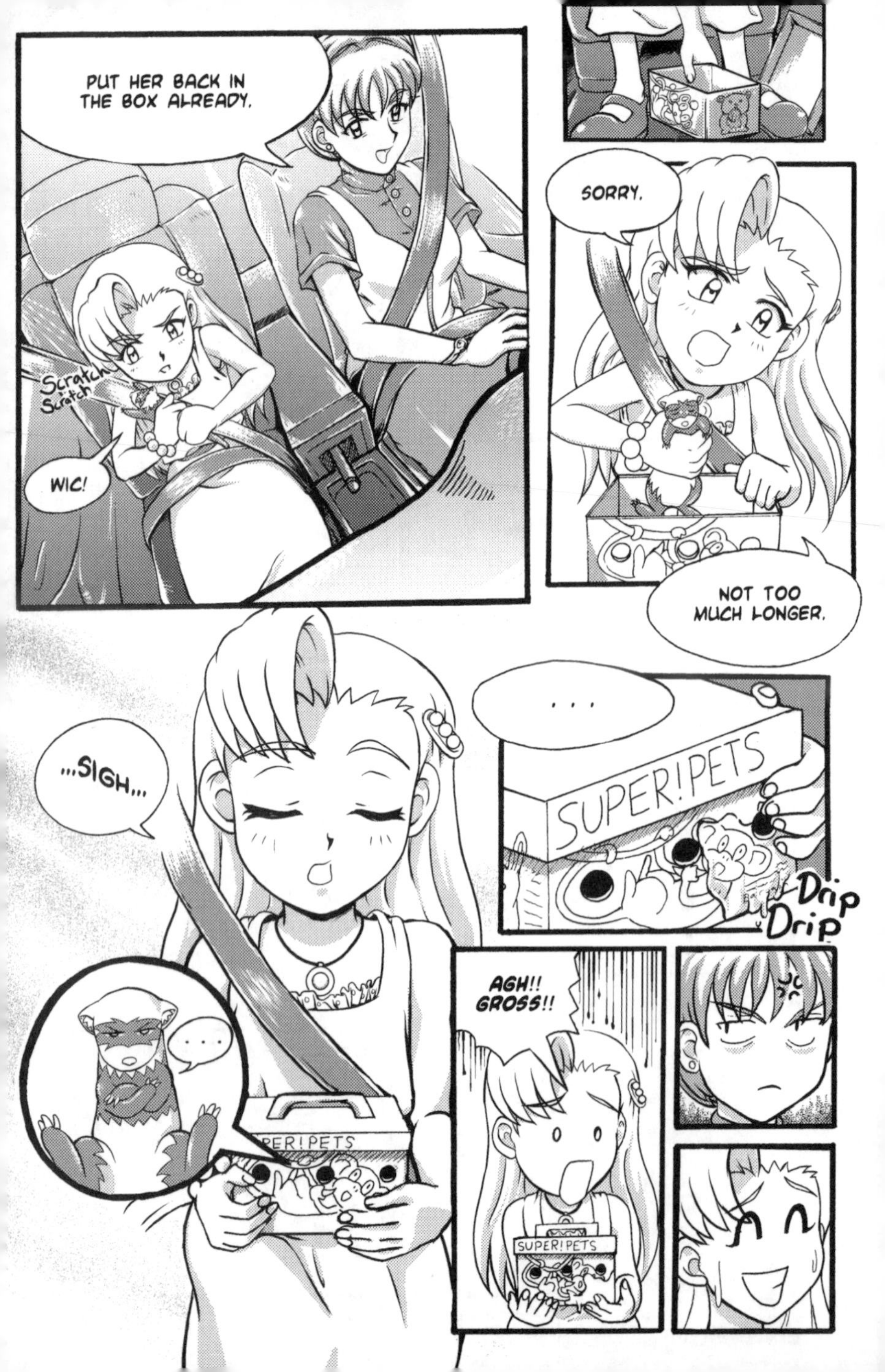
PUT HER BACK IN THE BOX ALREADY.
Scratch Scratch
WIC!
SORRY.
NOT TOO MUCH LONGER.
...SIGH...
. . .
. . .
SUPER!PETS
Drip Drip
AGH!! GROSS!!
SUPER!PETS

ERGH...
ALMOST HOME, FERRET...
HMM. FERRET.
Ferret's Qualities
1. Fuzzy
2. Smells interesting
. . .
BLESSED SHROOMS VEGETABLE MARKET
Peaches! Take one home!
AHA!
I'M GOING TO NAME HER...
PEACH!
BECAUSE SHE'S EXACTLY LIKE A PEACH. SHE FELT ALL FUZZY WHEN I WAS HOLDING HER.
HOW CLEVER.
A FUZZY PEACH?
COME ON, AMANDA...

SUPER!PETS
We're heeeeere!♡
MOMMY, MOMMY.
CAN I LET PEACH OUT SO SHE CAN SEE THE HOUSE?
SUPER!PETS
I SUPPOSE SO.
BUT JUST FOR A MOMENT. THEN WE'LL SET HER UP IN HER CAGE.

WELCOME HOME, PEACH!

DOOM
wh...where am I?
WHAT DO YOU THINK...
...PEACH?
DASH!
NO!
PEACH!
W--
WAIT!
scamper
CRASH!
THUNK!
WUD!
GRAB HER!

MEANWHILE...

SUPER!PETS
We have: cats dogs reptiles fish ferrets more!
GROOMING AND TRAINING: THURSDAY
PARROT
Uwileeeeeeee!
?
UWieeeeeeeeeeee
CLAP
SUPER! PETS
WHERE IS THAT NOISE COMING FROM?
Uwieeeeeee!!
OH MY GOSH! WHO PUT GUINEA PIGS IN THE FERRET CAGE??
heh heh heh heh
SUPER!PETS

REST
IN
PEACH

AWAKE YET, PEACH?
PROMISE TO BE ON YOUR BEST BEHAVIOR TODAY. MOM WAS REALLY ANGRY ABOUT THAT ESCAPE ACT YOU PULLED YESTERDAY...
IT'LL BE HARD FOR US TO BECOME GOOD FRIENDS IF I HAVE TO GO ALL THE WAY TO THE PET STORE TO VISIT YOU.
IT'S A GOOD THING YOU DIDN'T BREAK ANYTHING.
fwmp
hee~
blink
HEY,
srtch srtch
WANNA BE BRUSHED, TOO? LET'S MAKE YOU SHINE! MY FRIENDS ARE COMING OVER TODAY AND I WANT THEM TO LIKE YOU!

Chapter 2
R.I.P. van Ferret
ZANGOR

ENGLISH

Hiiiiiii Amanda!
HEY!
creak
HI!
SHUT
I THOUGHT SHE'D NEVER LET US GO UPSTAIRS. WE'VE BEEN STUCK DOWN THERE FOR LIKE, FOREVER, BEING FORCED TO LOOK AT HER MUSEUM OF ANTIQUES.
IT'S TRUE!
AND THAT VICTORIAN DRESS OF HERS! IT'S LIKE A FUNERAL! CREEPY!
nod nod
UH, SORRY. MOM GETS THAT WAY SOMETIMES WITH HER COLLECTION. I'LL WAIT BY THE FRONT DOOR NEXT TIME.
HERE! CHECK HER OUT! THIS IS WHAT I CALLED YOU OVER TO SEE!

HER NAME IS PEACH.
CUTE!
SHE'S A FERRET! SHE'S STILL A BABY, SO BE CAREFUL WITH HER 'CAUSE SHE'S DELICATE.
OKAY.
THIS IS THE COOLEST-LOOKING PET EVER! SHE'S LIKE A TINY SEAL WITH A RACCOON MASK. ...A SEAL-COON!
THUMBS UP!
Red HOT!
C-CAN IT DO ANY TRICKS?
POKE POKE
I DON'T KNOW... I HAVEN'T HAD HER LONG ENOUGH TO TRY ANYTHING YET.
walking upright
LET'S SEE...
Roll

AND HOW ABOUT...
WIC!!
toss

flump
gotcha!

NICE CATCH!
HA HA HA...

HisSSSSSsssSSSS

screech!
i'll...
i'll never bow to you, monster!
SHA-BOOM!
SHRIEEK!!
CHOMP!
YIKES!
WAUGH!

wick~~
THUD.

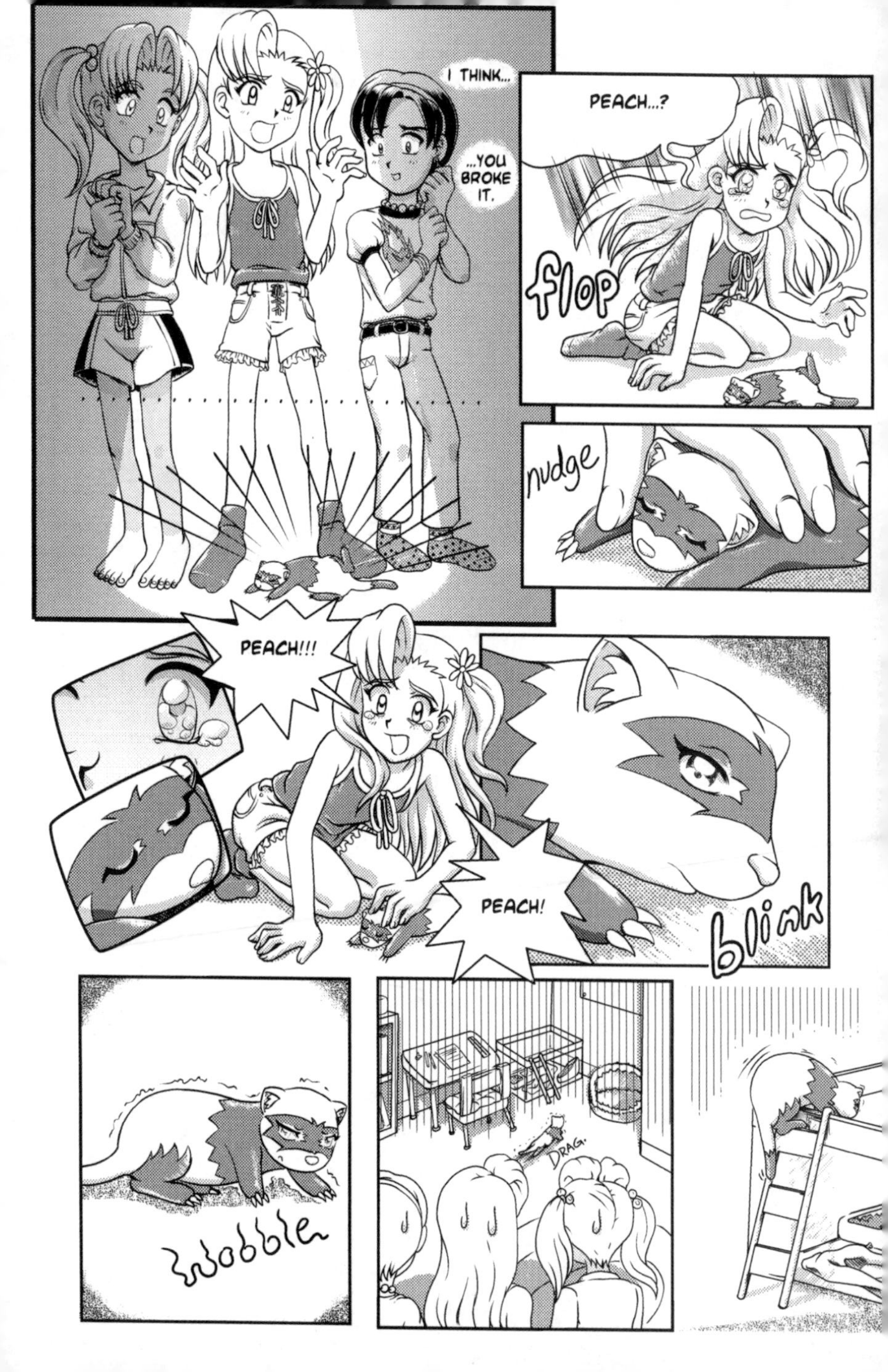
I THINK...
...YOU BROKE IT.
PEACH...?
flop
nudge
PEACH!!!
PEACH!
blink
wobble
DRAG.

...AND SHE'S OKAY!!
A-OK
. . .
I GUESS WE BETTER LEAVE PEACH ALONE FOR NOW.

YEAH...
. . .
HEY... LET'S GO OUTSIDE AND PLAY WITH YOUR FRISBEE.
IT'S BORING IN HERE.

...OKAY...
DON'T TELL MOM ABOUT WHAT HAPPENED.
OKAY?
OKAY.
YOU HAVE TO PROMISE!

STICK A NEEDLE IN MY EYE, EAT A POISON MUSHROOM 'TILL I DIE.
GOOD. LET'S GO.

ert
ert
ert
ert
ert
ert
ert
Click
SNOOZE
3:46
Alarm Clock
Good morning, peach!!
...STILL SLEEPING...?
PEACH?
nudge
Press
P-PEACH?
DROOP

tremble
tremble
tremble

Amanda...
WHY!?
why did you DROP meee?
I only wanted to be your friend

THUMP
THUMP
THUMP
THUMP
MOM!!
. . .
WHAT HAPPENED?
HOW CAN IT ALREADY BE DEAD?! THIS IS JUST MY LUCK! IT'S ONLY BEEN ONE DAY!!
Sniff
I-I DON'T KNOW!
OOOH, JUST PERFECT!
I DIDN'T DO ANYTHING!
GET DRESSED, AMANDA.

VROOSH
POOR PEACH. WE HAVE TO DO SOMETHING, MOMMY.
POOR MOM! THAT THING COST ME $120.
THEY'D BETTER TAKE IT BACK.
AMANDA, THERE'S NOTHING THE VET CAN DO. WE'RE TAKING HER BACK TO THE PET STORE TO GET YOU A NEW ONE.
TAKE HER BACK?!
WE'RE NOT GOING TO THE VET?
• • • • •

Sniff sniff
Please don't bury meeeee, You can save meeeee, Amanda...
Tell her! Tell her what you did to meeeee...
Sob
WAAAHH!
OKAY, OKAY!
I'LL SEE WHAT I CAN DO. HANG ON.

MUSHROOM
VALLEY
ANIMAL CLINIC
ORDER OF ANIMALS
MUSHROOM VALLEY
WELCOME

MUSHROOM
VALLEY
ANIMAL CLINIC
Walk-ins
WELCOME

EXIT
tac tic tkk

I CAN'T PLACE WHERE I'VE SEEN HER BEFORE, BUT SHE LOOKS FAMILIAR.

MOM!! HURRY!

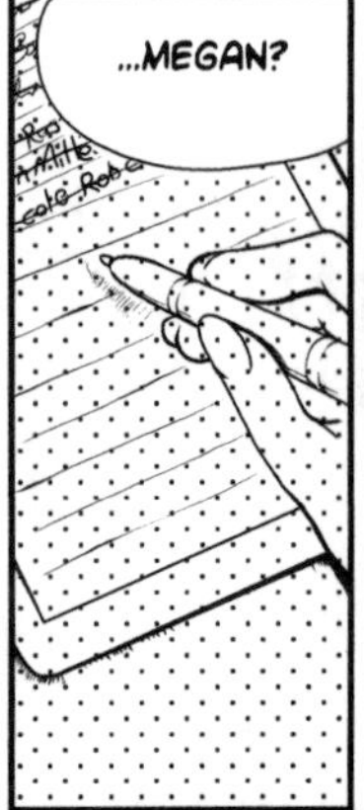
...MEGAN?

MEGAN KELLER?

I THOUGHT
IT WAS YOU.

...?

glance
Bridget Kross
MUSHROOM VALLEY
ANIMAL CLINIC

BRIDGET...?

REMEMBER ME? YOU HELPED ME FIND A HOUSE!
hmm

OH! OF COURSE!
I HAD NO IDEA THAT YOU WERE A VET, BRIDGET.

WEEEELL, I'M NOT, NOT YET.
I'M STILL IN SCHOOL, SO ALL I HANDLE IS PAPERWORK. BUT YOU KNOW... I NEVER GOT TO THANK YOU. I HAD AN APPRAISER COME OUT, AND YOU KNOW...

...YOU SAVED ME A FORTUNE ON THAT HOUSE! I REALLY OWE YOU ONE!
IT WAS NO BIG DEAL. BESIDES, WE SINGLE MOMS NEED TO STICK TOGETHER.
SOOOOO...
WHAT CAN WE DO FOR YOU TODAY?
smile
WELL, MY DAUGHTER'S FERRET...
A FERRET? THAT'S DIFFERENT. WHERE DID YOU GET IT?
UH.
THAT PET STORE NEARBY.
PETCETERA?
NO, THE OTHER ONE.
TUG TUG
ANIMAL HOUSE?

NO.
IT'S THE ONE ON MUSHROOM GROVES DRIVE.
"SUPER!PETS".
EXIT
REALLY?
THAT'S A NICE SHOP FOR A NON-CHAIN STORE. THEY'RE SMALL, BUT...

WHAT DID YOU THINK OF THE CLERK WHO WORKS THERE?
whisper

THE SUPER!PETS STORE CLERK...?
SUPER!PETS

A BIT OUTRAGEOUS, BUT NOT TOO BAD, RIGHT?
WINK

EH HEH HEH HEH.
MOOOOM!!
TUG!
PEACH, REMEMBER?

RIGHT! SO ANYWAY, ABOUT MY DAUGHTER'S FERRET.
STARE
GRRRR
IF IT'S NOT TOO BIG OF A DEAL, CAN YOU MAYBE CHECK AND SEE IF IT'S...
...IT'S DEAD?
MOOOOM!
PEACH ISN'T DEAD.
WE JUST GOT HER.
MAY I SEE THE FERRET?
...
I CAN TRY CHECKING HER VITAL SIGNS.

tug
Poke poke
...
fwoosh
WHAT HAPPENED TO HER?
SHE'S ALIVE, BUT...
...HER HEARTBEAT IS VERY FAINT!

I...

........

SUFFF

MURDERER!

...DON'T KNOW!!
SOB!

SOB
SOB

FWUMP!
WHOA THERE, LITTLE LADY!
SEE, BRIDGET? ♡
WOMEN CAN'T SEEM TO KEEP THEIR HANDS OFF ME. HA HA HA!
COUGH
DOCTOR!
PLEASE LOOK AT THEIR FERRET.
IT'S BARELY BREATHING!
AREN'T YOU A LUCKY LADY.
I HAVE AN OPENING RIGHT NOW. FOLLOW ME.
SCRF
LUCKY? HOW'S IT LUCKY TO HAVE A DYING FERRET?!
DON'T WORRY, SWEETIE.
I'LL TAKE GOOD CARE OF YOUR PET. I'M ONE OF THE BEST VETS AROUND.

NO OFFENSE...
...BUT THIS IS ONE UGLY CAT!
PEACH IS A FERRET.
OH.
RIGHT. GOTCHA.
PRESS
twitch
blink
yawn!!
?? ?? ??

It's a Miracle
PEACH!
SHE SEEMS OKAY NOW.
IT APPEARS THAT ALL SHE NEEDED WAS THE EXPERT CARE AND HANDLING OF A MASTER VET.
heh
WHAT WAS WRONG WITH HER?!

I HAVE NO IDEA.

I JUST DEAL WITH DOGS AND CATS.

WE DON'T GENERALLY DEAL WITH--

CHOMP

WILD AND EXOTIC CREATURES.
IT BIT ME!! THIS THING BETTER HAVE ALL ITS RABIES SHOTS!

VALLEY
ANIMAL CLINIC
Patient info:
owner: megan keller
Pet name: "Peach"
pet type: cat dog other
Birthdate: 6/2
sex: female
Height: 8 in long
weight: .5 lbs
Problem: unconscious ferret, difficulty breathing.
course of treatment:
ferret fine. Classic case of an exhausted baby animal. Overanxious owners. Bill them for the cost of a full exam
MVAC: we care
I WILL VENTURE A GUESS THAT YOUR FERRET WAS JUST TIRED.
OKAY! YOU'RE GOOD TO GO.
TH-THAT'S IT?
THAT'S IT. HAVE A NICE DAY, AND TAKE CARE OF YOUR LITTLE FERRET.
We Woo!!
THANKS FOR THE HELP, BRIDGET. IT TURNS OUT THAT THE FERRET WAS JUST FINE.
THAT'S WONDERFUL, MEGAN! COME VISIT US AGAIN SOON, OKAY?
WELL, HOPEFULLY NOT TOO SOON! HA HA HA HA.
hahaha!
HAHAHA...

UH...
HEY, HEY! HANG ON A MOMENT. DON'T FORGET TO PAY YOUR BILL!

BILL?! JUST FOR LOOKING AT THE FERRET?!

smile
$50.00
fwp

THIS IS HALF THE COST OF THE STUPID ANIMAL. RIDICULOUS!
WHAT ABOUT OWING ME ONE? I SAVED THAT WOMAN THOUSANDS OF DOLLARS!

THANK YOU, MOMMY! YOU SAVED PEACH!!

EVEN THOUGH IT'LL BE A MAJOR DRAIN ON OUR FINANCES...
FOR AMANDA'S SAKE, I SUPPOSE IT'S WORTH IT.

fwp
fwp
Page 1 of 3
Account Statement
MUSHROOM VALLEY BANK
SUPER!PETS
Fuzzy farm feed
Kitty litter 35.49
10.99
total 45.98
tax 3.22
49.20
HONEY... WE NEED TO TALK.
...COMING UP NEXT ON AFTERNOON TOONS...
OKAY...

YOUR FERRET.
IT'S PUT SOME STRAIN ON THE FAMILY FINANCES WITH ALL THE EXPENSES IT'S RACKED UP SO FAR.
UH HUH?

CAGE, FOOD, TREATS, TOYS, SUPPLIES, LITTER, THAT VET VISIT...

AMANDA, ARE YOU LISTENING TO ME?!
click
YES, MOOOOM.

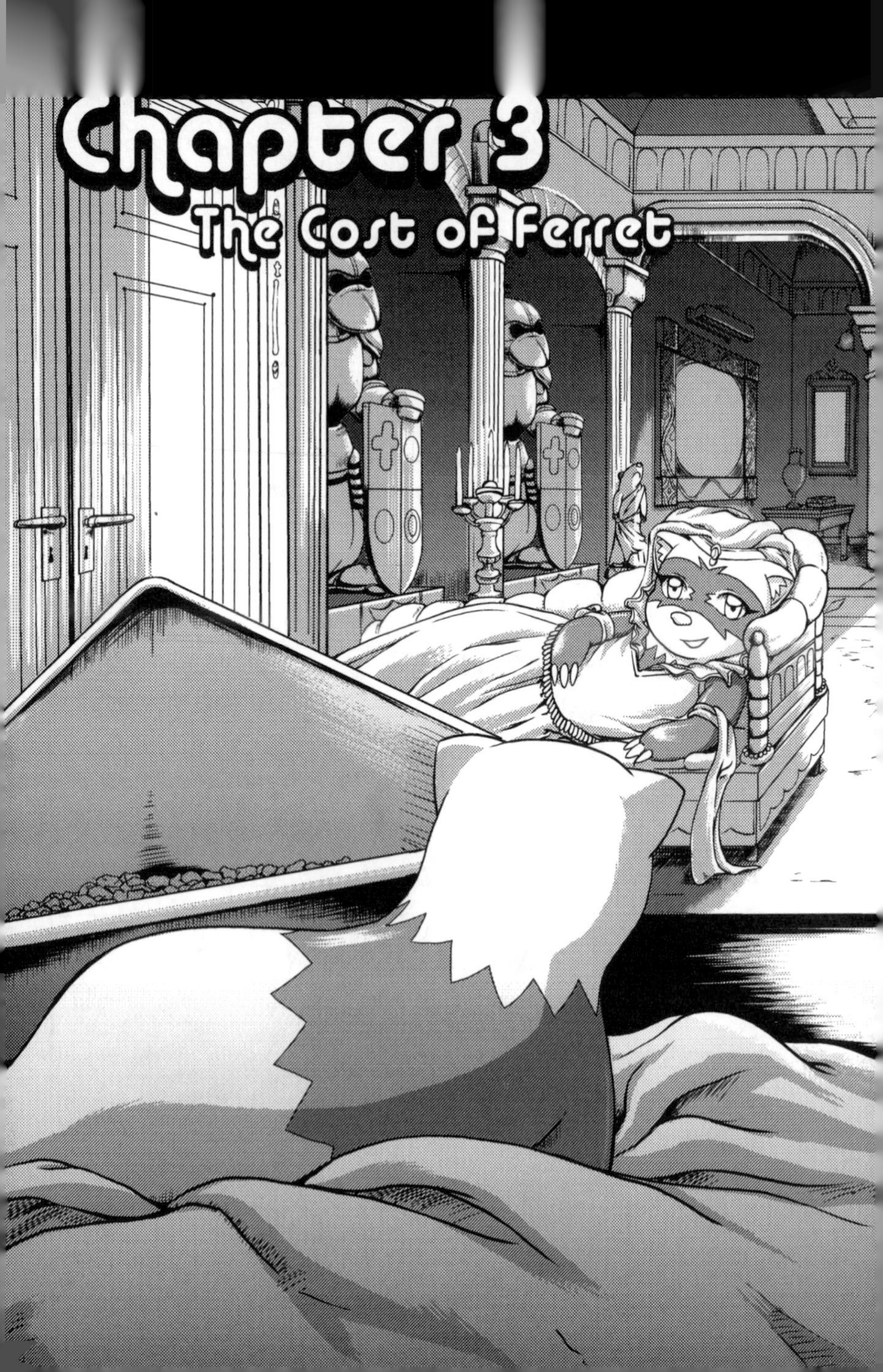
Chapter 3
The Cost of Ferret

sigh...
this is no life for a princess.

perhaps i could find a way out of the handra's lair and back to my kingdom.

...
Press

no monsters on guard right now.
seems like an opportune time to escape.

glance
hmm.

PUSH
shsh

HRMPH!
Scrape
Scrape

fwump
Dash
that was laughably simple!
not surprising, considering my physical and mental prowess!
wish i tried that sooner.

Bounce
Bounce

!
THMP

oh!
my first
royal
subject!
greetings,
peasant!
my name
is peach.
skitter
hey!!
wait!
Bug

how DARE
you turn your
back on me!
i'm your new
prin--
fwump

...cess...

$20 FOR A BAG OF FOOD.
$10 FOR LITTER.
. . .
I REALLY DON'T UNDERSTAND WHY AN ANIMAL THREE TIMES SMALLER THAN A CAT COSTS THREE TIMES AS MUCH!!
THE STORE CLERK TOLD ME FERRETS WERE SUPPOSED TO BE LIKE LITTLE CATS IN CAGES!
Meow ♡
click
UH HUH.
A FISH WOULD HAVE BEEN A BETTER CHOICE.
CLEANER... CHEAPER...
RATHER THAN LAYING AROUND CHANNEL-SURFING, YOU SHOULD BE UPSTAIRS PLAYING WITH THAT FERRET!

OR ARE YOU ALREADY BORED WITH IT?!
Shuffle~
THUMP
THUMP
THUMP
THUMP
Thump
Thump

...
I WAS TOO HARD ON HER. SHE'S NOT EVEN OLD ENOUGH TO UNDERSTAND THE VALUE OF MONEY YET.
thump
thump
thump
...SHOULD'VE BEEN MORE GENTLE.

AMANDA? HONEY?
...OH DEAR...
Waaugh!!

srch
LOOK, ABOUT EARLIER.
WHAT?!
SHE MUST HAVE HEARD YOU AND DECIDED TO LEAVE THE FAMILY!
Sob
MOOOOOOM, I CAN'T FIND PEACH ANYWHERE!

HON--
scrtch
scrtch
?
scrtch
HOW DID YOU ESCAPE?!
WICK!

SUPER!PETS
EXOT
PET
SP G
We have: cats dogs reptiles fish ferrets more!
GROOMING AND TRAINING THURSDAY
PARROT SALE
WE CARE
SUPER!PETS
I'M SORRY, BUT...
...SUPER!PETS' RETURN POLICY PREVENTS ME FROM ACCEPTING USED MERCHANDISE.
SUPER!PETS

WE'VE HAD THIS FISH TANK FOR LESS THAN A WEEK!
pat pat
big heavy rock.
spare plywood.
masking tape.
fish tank.
suffocating ferret.
IT'S HARDLY USED.

MA'AM.
oook oook
YOU ARE CURRENTLY HOUSING A FERRET IN THAT CAGE. THEREFORE, IT'S USED.
thump
SUPER!PETS
scr tch scr tch

Scrtch
Scrtch

hard...
to
breathe...

must...
get...
out...

blink
!

WOOOOOOOO

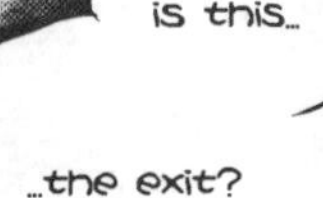
is this...
...the exit?
step step

mommy-ferret!
you'll always be
my little princess...

LOOK.

THIS WOULDN'T BE USED MERCHANDISE...
THUMP
...IF YOUR STORE HAD SOLD ME THE RIGHT CAGE IN FIRST PLACE.

MA'AM, I APOLOGIZE...
OOK OOK!
...BUT THE OTHER CLERK MADE THAT MISTAKE.
SUPER! PETS

AND BETWEEN YOU AND ME, SHE LACKS THE HEART OF A TRUE ANIMAL LOVER. THE BOSS JUST HIRED HER AS EYE CANDY.
OOK
SUPER! PETS

OTHER CLERK?! SO THIS IS THE CLERK BRIDGET WAS TALKING ABOUT!
BUT THIS IRRESPONSIBLE JERK IS HARDLY WHAT I'D CALL A GOOD CATCH.

OH, FORGET IT. JUST SHOW ME SOME CAGES THAT WILL HOLD A FERRET.

SURE!
WE HAVE SEVERAL TO CHOOSE FROM.
ook ook
SUPER!PETS
Travel Critter
The perfect starter kit for taking home your new little animal. Helps the critter adjust to its surroundings!
$40.00
TRAVEL CRITTER
$80.00
FERRET CONDO
Ferret Condo
Your growing ferret will love this quaint little one-bedroom home.
Ferret essentials
16 SUPER!PETS Catalog
Ferret Mansion
Because they deserve the best! Treat your ferrets to a life of luxury. Three floors, escape tube, two hammocks, self-cleaning litter box, and more!
SUPER!PETS
Best Buy!
FERRET MANSION
$200.00
Ferret essentials
SUPER!PETS Catalog 17
HMM.
tap
THAT ONE.
ABSOLUTELY NOT!
ook!
tok
SUPER! PET

I'M SORRY, BUT I WILL NOT SELL YOU THAT CAGE. IT'S FAR TOO SMALL TO HOUSE A GROWING FERRET.
OOK!
QUITE FRANKLY, FORCING AN ANIMAL TO ENDURE THAT WOULD BE TANTAMOUNT TO ANIMAL ABUSE.
OOK!
WHY OFFER IT IF IT'S TOO SMALL?
MA'AM, I'LL HAVE TO CALL THE ASPCA IF YOU CONTINUE TO ARGUE THIS MATTER!
THAT CAGE IS FORBIDDEN! PICK A DIFFERENT ONE.
OKAY, OKAY, FINE.
I'LL TAKE THAT ONE, THEN.

WHY?
IS THIS ONE TOO SMALL, TOO?
Ook!
HMM. I DON'T KNOW. YOU'D BE BETTER OFF GOING FOR ONE SIZE UP.
IT'S ALL RIGHT FOR JUST ONE FERRET, BUT NO ONE BUYS JUST ONE.
WHAT?!
FERRETS AREN'T LIKE CATS OR DOGS.
IT ISN'T SATISFYING TO JUST OWN ONE. YOU'LL BE BACK FOR ANOTHER FERRET OR TWO... OR THREE.
TRUST ME.
heeee~
glance

STEP
MOMMY?
hehe
NO!!
ONE IS ENOUGH FOR US.
I'LL TAKE THE MEDIUM CAGE.
VERY WELL. WHILE I'M GETTING THAT...
ook!

WHY NOT PICK OUT SOME FISH FOR YOURSELF?
OOK OOK
HUH?

YOUR FISH TANK! YOU MIGHT AS WELL PUT SOMETHING IN IT.
fish Paradise
UH...
I RECOMMEND OUR TROPICAL FISH.

THEY'RE SCIENTIFICALLY PROVEN TO REDUCE STRESS LEVELS.
...

WOULD YOU LIKE A BROTHER OR SISTER, PEACH?
NO ONE GETS JUST OOOOOONNNEEE!
blub blub blub blub
. . . . .
$200 WORTH OF TROPICAL FISH TO FEED AND CARE FOR.
blub blub
SO MUCH MONEY. I HATE THIS. I HATE THESE FISH. I ESPECIALLY HATE THE FERRET THAT STARTED THIS MESS.

SHOW
tck tck
DON'T FORGET, CLASS...
tck tck tck
NEXT FRIDAY IS SHOW AND TELL. START THINKING ABOUT WHAT YOU WANT TO BRING IN.

NOW,
glance
Scrtch
BEFORE THE BELL RINGS, I'D LIKE TO PASS BACK YOUR SPELLING TEST.

A BIG CONGRATS TO BOTH AMANDA KELLER AND KIM CHANG ON ACHIEVING YOUR THIRD "A" IN A ROW!
HELP YOURSELVES TO A PRIZE FROM THE TREASURE CHEST!

HE'S SO CUTE! HE'LL LOOK GREAT ON MY WINDOW SILL. ♡
RIGHT ON!
SAVE
Snicker
heh

DO YOU WANT A THIRD CHECK BY YOUR NAME, PHIL?
HA! HOW FITTING.
AN UGLY TOY FOR AN UGLY GIRL!
SHUT UP, PHIL!
HA HA HA
SLUMP
SAVE ME

Chapter 4
Gladiator Peach

thump
Thump
THUMP
cla-chk

BAM
tok

STUPID PHIL. ALWAYS PICKING ON ME...
fwUmp
PEACH, I'M GOING OVER TO KIM'S HOUSE TONIGHT.

NOT THAT YOU'D NOTICE SINCE YOU'RE ALWAYS SLEEPING.
fwp
rustle rustle

UGH.
HERE! I DON'T WANT THIS UGLY THING, SO YOU CAN HAVE IT.

IT'LL KEEP YOU COMPANY WHILE I'M GONE.
:hmp:
THUMP!
srshsshhshhsshhhh
?
Spring
no! wait!
Urf!
Slam

i command you to release me!
scrape scrape

!
Sniff

who are you?
how long have you been watching me?

Smile

don't act so familiar with me, peasant!

off my blanket! and wipe that silly smile off your face!
Smack!

flump

i don't know why the monsters trapped you in here with me...
...but since they have...
...i will lay out the law of my kingdom for you.

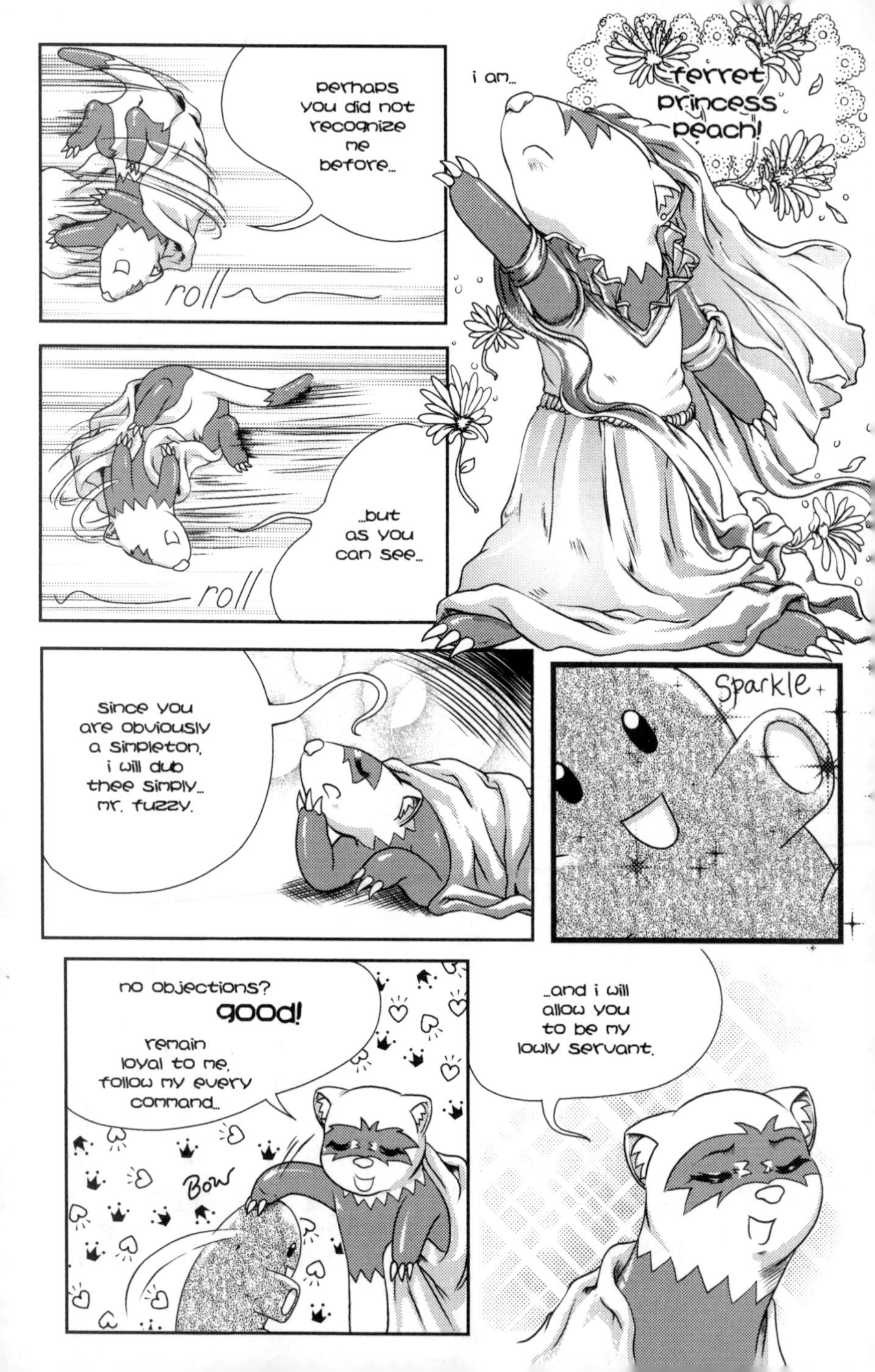
perhaps you did not recognize me before...
roll
...but as you can see...
roll
i am...
ferret princess peach!
since you are obviously a simpleton, i will dub thee simply... mr. fuzzy.
Sparkle
...and i will allow you to be my lowly servant.
no objections? good!
remain loyal to me, follow my every command...
Bow

BYE, PEACH.
CLICK

. . .

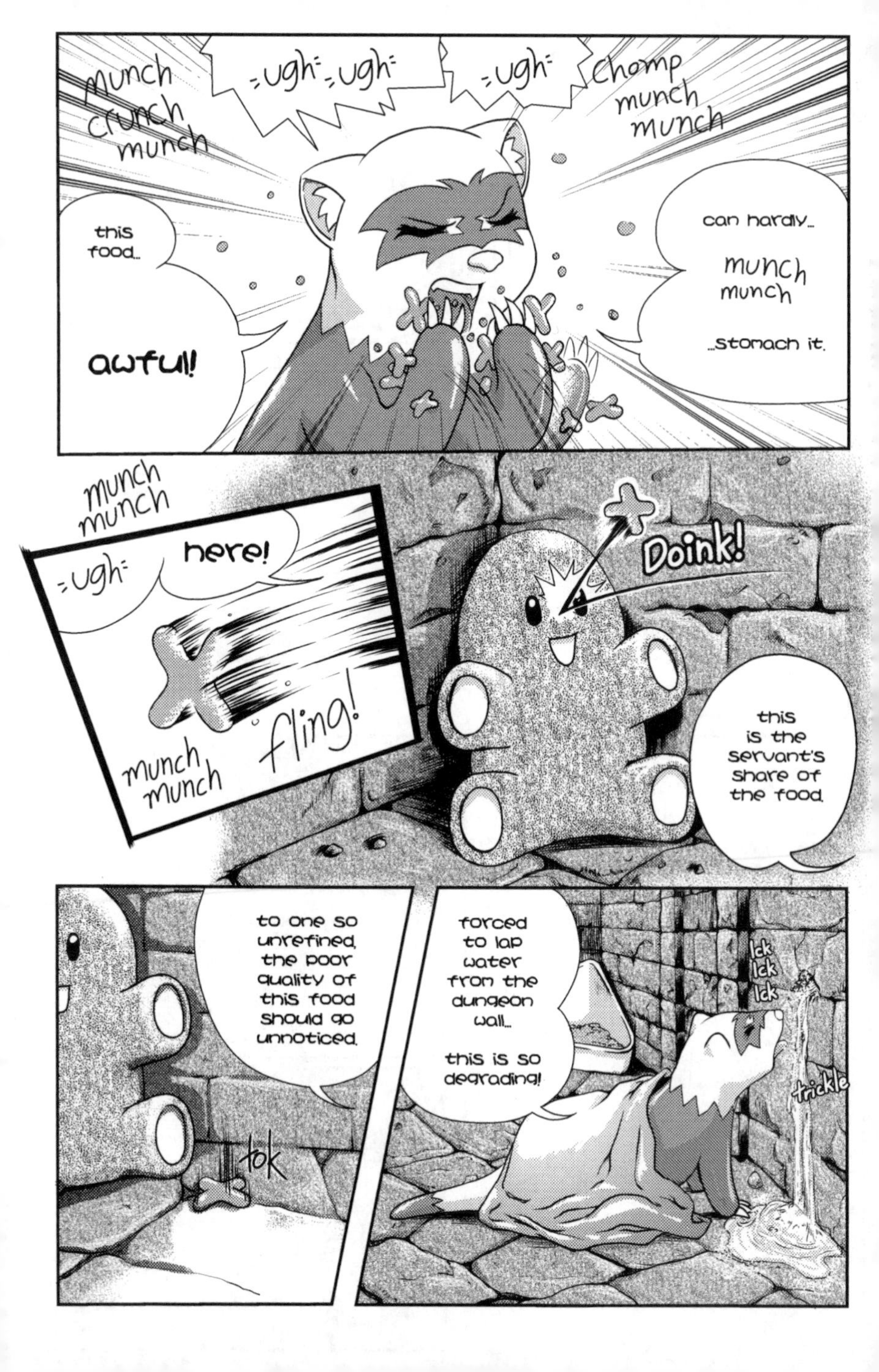
munch crunch munch
ugh ugh
ugh
Chomp munch munch
this food...
awful!
can hardly...
munch munch
...stomach it.
munch munch
ugh
here!
fling!
munch munch
Doink!
this is the servant's share of the food.
to one so unrefined, the poor quality of this food should go unnoticed.
tok
forced to lap water from the dungeon wall...
this is so degrading!
lck lck lck
trickle

. . . . . .
shuffle

this is so humiliating.
stop staring at me! have you no shame?!

tsk!
i appreciate your vigilance, but there are times when a watchful eye is NOT needed.
step

the handra does not often attack at night.
so you may relax your guard now.

Yawn!

...if you insist on keeping watch all night, i...

what's that?

mr. fuzzy... were you saving this kibble for me?

Smile

he's staying awake to protect me!
Munch crunch

BLUSH

Snooze

...SLEEPING AGAIN.
HOW BORING.
MAKE HER DO SOMETHING.
srshssh~~

srshhhhshh

shriekk!

you toss and turn too much, mr. fuz—

tremble

HIYA, PEACH! LEARN ANY NEW TRICKS?
LOOKING COOL, SEAL-COON!
WHICH REMINDS ME... YOU'VE GOT TO TAKE HER TO SHOW-AND-TELL, AMANDA!
I'VE BEEN THINKING ABOUT IT...
BUT... WHAT IF PHIL MAKES FUN OF ME AGAIN?
HA HA HA HA
HA HA HA! AN UGLY ANIMAL FOR AN UGLY GIRL!
YOU REALLY NEED TO TOUGHEN UP!
THEY WOULDN'T PICK ON YOU IF YOU FOUGHT BACK.

Squeeze
YOU DON'T HAVE TO PUT UP WITH ANY MEANIE ATTACKS.

EVEN A SEAL-COON KNOWS HOW TO DEFEND ITSELF.
Seal-coon

fling
FWUMP
WATCH THIS!
The Arena

wick!
tickle tickle

how dare you, monsters!
AROooo

AROooo...
AROoooo...
SNAP
SNAP
WOW! SHE'S WILD TODAY!
ka-pow!
DODGE
PUNT
shrieekk
Slither
Retreat!
Retreat!!
hmp!
Slither
Slither

humph!
cower before your rightful princess!
HER LITTLE BITES KINDA HURT.
GOT SOMETHING ELSE WE CAN USE?
PEER
hello there, peasant...
i thank you for coming to my aid. however, i am no longer in need of rescue.

Pop!
what?!
how dare you?!
fskk
fskk
?
WA-POW
K.O.

WUMP! x8
CREK
SNPP
SNPP
CRREK
CRRROAR
BUSH!

. . .
CRRK
DOOM

SCREECH!
why is this creature after me?!
SNAP
SNAP
SNAP
it's under the control of the handra!
so that's what's going on!

Dash
Snip Snip
Snip Snip
no! trapped!
we don't have to fight!
stop now and i'll still allow you to become one of my royal subjects.
ROAR
no!!
don't let these cruel monsters control you. together, we can fight against them!

TOKK
RR
ROAR
can nothing get through that thick shell of yours?!
you leave me no choice.
fling
WICK!
?
yank!
YOW! SHE TOTALLY YANKED THAT TOY OUT OF MY HAND.
GO PEACH GO!
I THINK SHE DESERVES A TREAT.
Slam

i'm sorry...
The Victor

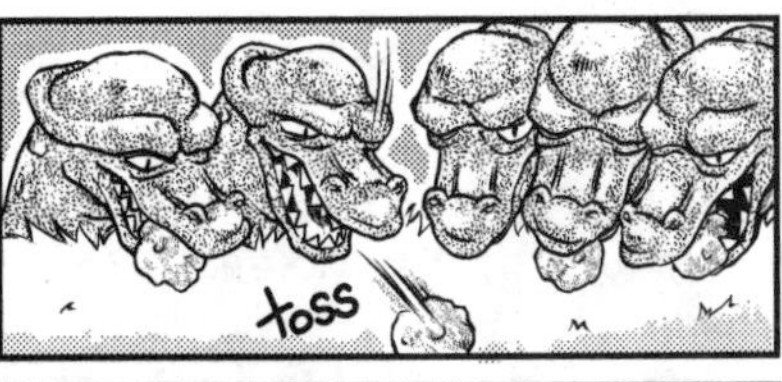
toss

?
THUNK

sniff~
wonderful aroma.

munch munch munch
delicious! amazing! truly gourmet food worthy of a delicate princess' palate.

should i save one for mr. fuzzy?

tch, no.
he failed me like the others.
plus these delectables are too refined for a simple peasant.

toss
was the food a reward for fighting the claw monster...?

. . .
munch chew

i can't allow myself to become a source of amusement for those vile handra.

Snatch
hurk!

hiss
TOSS
thud

rub rub
ow! ow! . . .

glance
staring at me again, jealous about the treat, no doubt.

don't give me that look! let's not forget who fell asleep during guard duty.
Step Step

how much longer can i endure this? oh mommy-ferret, what shall become of me?

Chapter 5
Biting Terror

for as long as I can remember...
Swhp
ffwp
...i've been fighting in the arena.
. . .
rigorous gladiator training where my strength is tested against the strength of the other warriors.
unfortunately, necessity has required me to shed my princess gown for a suit of armor.

ONE OF THE MORE CHALLENGING ADVERSARIES CAME IN THE FORM OF A DEEP-SEA TERROR... A GREAT WHITE... MR. SHARK!
TWO ROWS OF RAZOR SHARP TEEETH!
INCREDIBLE AGILITY!
A MASSIVE, MUSCULAR FRAME!
AS HE MOVED IN FOR THE KILL, SMASHING THROUGH THE DOCK, HIS VICTORY SEEMED INEVITABLE.
HOWEVER, HE MISCALCULATED HIS LANDING AND FELL UPON MY SWORD.

ANOTHER OPPONENT I CAN REMEMBER CLEARLY... MR. BEAR.
WE FOUGHT DEEP WITHIN HIS DOMAIN... THE DARK FOREST OF NO RETURN.
HE NAVIGATED THE COMPLEX MAZE OF TREES WITH EASE.
TO MAKE MATTERS WORSE, MY SWORD COULD NOT PENETRATE HIS THICK, COARSE FUR.
IN THE END, MY SPEED AND STAMINA ALLOWED ME TO REMAIN ONE STEP AHEAD OF HIM.
WEARY FROM EXHAUSTION, HE SMASHED HEADFIRST INTO A TREE AND BROUGHT A RAIN OF DEBRIS TUMBLING DOWN UPON HIM.

THE DAINTY NO-FUR PROVED TO BE SURPRISINGLY DEADLY. WHAT SHE LACKED IN STRENGTH, SHE MADE UP FOR IN CUNNING.
SHE DISARMED ME WITH HER GENTLE SMILE AND AN ARMFUL OF DELICIOUS TREATS. I LOWERED MY GUARD WHILE I FEASTED.
BUT THEN A SHARP PAIN SHOT THROUGH ME AS THE HEEL OF HER SHOE CONNECTED WITH MY SIDE.
THEN SHE LEAPT UPON ME TO STRANGLE ME WITH HER TALONED CLAWS.
IN THE END, I MANAGED TO KICK HER OFF ME AND SENT HER FLYING INTO THE MANSION BEHIND US.
SHE COLLAPSED IN A PILE OF CURLY HAIR AND FRILLY DRESS.

after every battle...
...there was only mr. fuzzy to welcome me back and comfort me.

sigh
because i am a princess, i can not acknowledge you as more than my servant, but you are truly special to me.
munch munch
thank you, mr. fuzzy.

and then the day came when all the gladiators had been defeated, except one...
Srshhhhh
that useless servant!
how dare he disappear right before a battle?
keep your distance, i'm going!
Shaaaaa
hiss!
...

WHOOSH
BOOM
Wobble

you!
. . . !
AWOOOOOOOOOOO
but why?!

fwoom

VROOSH

THUD
THUD
AROOOOOOOO

WHY ARE YOU ATTACKING ME?

THUD
THUD

SWOOO

RIPP
AGHH!
RRIPP

Fssh
AROOooo
i'm...sorry! are you angry because i never shared any of the treats with you?
no, this cuts much deeper. why didn't i realize it sooner?
for him to change so drastically...
AWOOooo
WHUD WHUD
then... this, this is... punishment for everyone i've mistreated in my life!
WHUD
it must be because i've treated mr. fuzzy like a slave, even though he's been so good to me.

ROOARrr
Aghhh!
squeeze
crackk
this is justice for all the injustices i've placed upon others. a fitting end for a tragic princess.
KNEEL, PEASANTS!
no, wait!
this isn't right!
I'm a princess
it's my right and privilege to be pampered!
Shriekk!
how dare mr. fuzzy expect exceptional treatment?!

thank you
for showing me
how important
i am, mommy-ferret!

Jhnnn~
Chomp!

SWOSH
POP
glance
ptoo

m-mr fuzzy?!
oh, no!
no, no, no!
i didn't want to hurt you! i was only fighting for survival!
OH POO. HE'LL HAVE TO BE REPAIRED.
SWOOP
hiss
handra! you're the ones to blame!
pitting us against each other.
i never wanted to be a gladiator. you forced me to become one!
SHRIEK!
CHOMP
WAUGHH
?

WHAT'S WRONG? WHAT HAPPENED?

IF IT BITES YOU, WE'RE TAKING IT BACK!
Sniff
N-NOTHING. I UH... SMASHED MY FINGER IN THE CLOSET...
THE CLOSET DOOR!

. . .
Suspiciously angry ferret

LET ME SEE.
ouch ouch ouch
yank

Bite Marks!!

WE'RE TAKING HER BACK!

WE WON'T TAKE HER BACK.
WE CAN TAKE BACK THE MERCHANDISE IF IT'S UNUSED. 75% RESTOCKING FEE, OF COURSE. ♡
Below the counter
BUT NOT THE FERRET. IT'S A LIVING CREATURE, AND IT'S LIKELY TO HAVE ALREADY IMPRINTED ON YOUR FAMILY.
Co♪
WOULDN'T IT BE TERRIBLE TO BREAK UP THE FAMILY?
MOM!!
THAT FERRET ISN'T PART OF OUR FAMILY.
LOOK AT WHAT IT DID!

AH, SO THAT'S THE PROBLEM...
LOW PRICES
SUPER!PETS
SUPER!PETS
EASILY FIXED.
SEE, ALL KITS NIP. YOUR LITTLE ONE JUST NEEDS SOME PROPER DISCIPLINE TO TEACH IT THAT BITING IS A BAD HABIT.
WE HAVE THIS FANTASTIC PRODUCT THAT'LL-
BAM
COO
PER!PETS
NO MORE FERRET MERCHANDISE!
OKAY, OKAY, UNDERSTOOD.
I HAVE ANOTHER SOLUTION.

HEY THERE, LITTLE TROUBLE-MAKER.
SUPER PETS
hmm
SCRUFF
POP
THIS SIMULATES THE NATURAL DISCIPLINARY ACTION OF A MOMMY FERRET.
TO TRANSPORT ITS BABIES, THE MOMMY DRAGS THEM BY THE SCRUFF OF THEIR NECK.
SRSh
BY SCRUFFING, THE FERRET WILL COME TO ACCEPT YOU AS THE MOMMY.

LET ME SHOW YOU ANOTHER TECHNIQUE.
CHOMP
SMACK
SUPE
wick!
TS
gasp
A LITTLE SPANK ON THE REAR SHOWS IT THAT BITING IS UNACCEPTABLE AND WILL ONLY CAUSE ITSELF PAIN.
AND IF THAT STILL DOESN'T WORK...
grrrr
Biting with all her might

THERE'S ONE OTHER THING YOU COULD TRY.
Ready
Aim.
grrr
THUMP
wick
ABSOLUTELY NOT!
I DON'T BELIEVE IN CORPORAL PUNISHMENT!
AH, THERE'S THE RELEASE!
SUPER!PETS
~whimper
wick
A FLICK ON THE NOSE TENDS TO DO THE TRICK. IT'S ALL A MATTER OF ASSERTING YOURSELF AS BOSS.
WANT TO TRY?
whimper
I DON'T DO IT TO AMANDA. I'M NOT GOING TO DO IT TO PEACH!

...
HMMM. I DON'T KNOW WHAT I CAN TELL YOU THEN. IF DISCIPLINE WON'T DO...
...
UNCOM-FORTABLE SILENCE
...AND YOU DIDN'T WANT THE ANTI-BITE PRODUCT...
ER... ABOUT THAT...
grin
THIS IS "BITTER BITE" SPRAY. THE BITE THAT BITES BOTH WAYS!
IT HAS A REPULSIVELY BITTER TASTE. THE FERRET WON'T WANT TO BITE ANYTHING THAT TASTES LIKE THIS SPRAY. TRUST ME.
AND BEST OF ALL? IT'S NON-TOXIC, COMPLETELY SAFE.
BITTER BITE!
Punish bad ferrets!
The bite that BITES BACK!
SUPER!PETS

SLAM
YAAAY!! PEACH IS HOME!
Spill
THUMP THUMP THUMP
HOW DID THAT GUY MANAGE TO CONVINCE ME TO BUY ALL THIS JUNK?!
FUZZY FARMS
KITTY LITTER
MORE MORE
"BITTER BITE" BETTER WORK...

PACE
PACE
PACE
censored
Step
Step
FWUMP

Chapter 6
Reforming Peach

fuzzy farms feed
WITH REAL CHICKEN!
FOR ACTIVE FERRETS

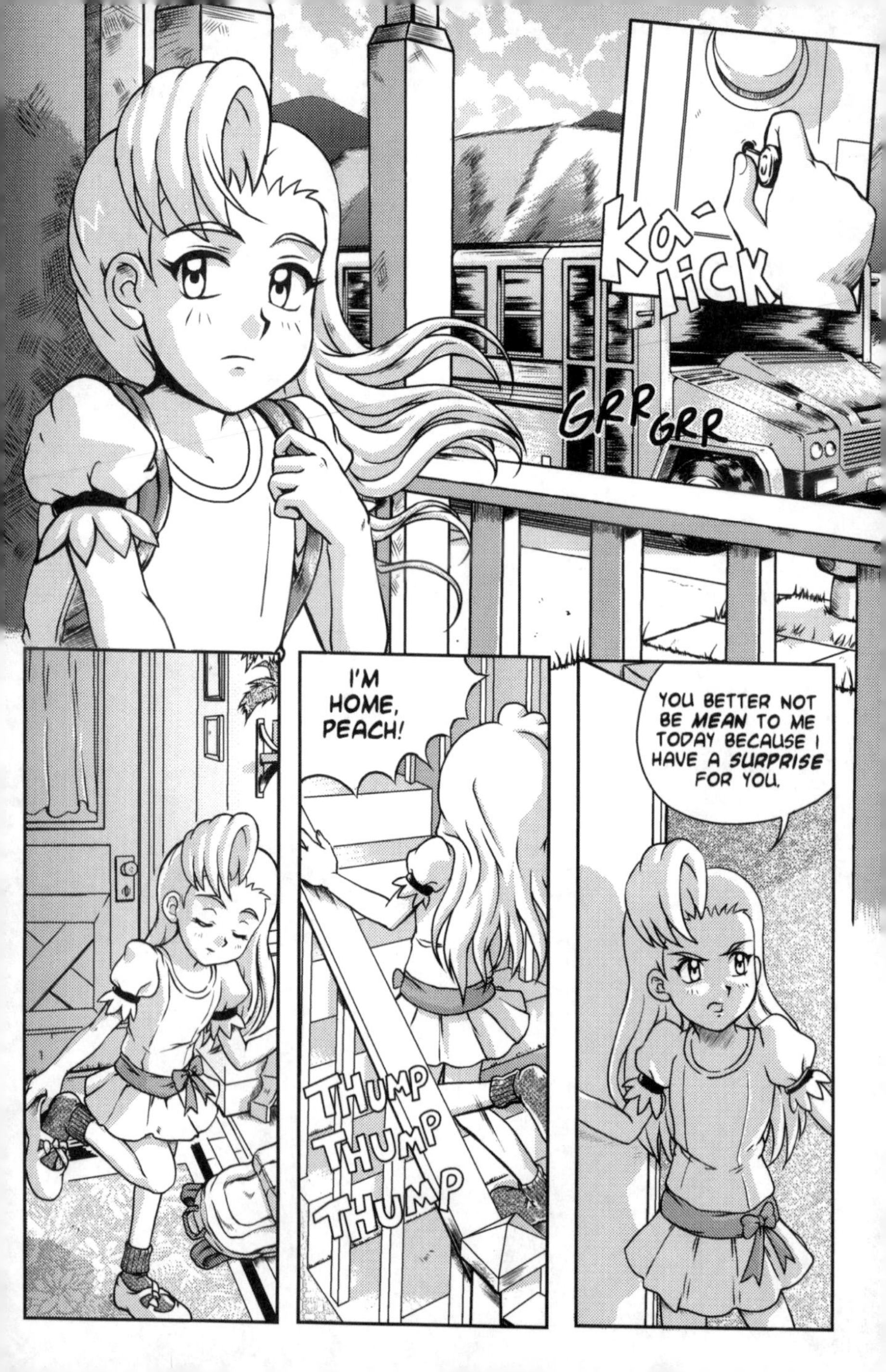
KA-LICK
GRR GRR
I'M HOME, PEACH!
THUMP THUMP THUMP
YOU BETTER NOT BE MEAN TO ME TODAY BECAUSE I HAVE A SURPRISE FOR YOU.

WAIT 'TIL YOU SEE! "AUNTIE" KIM HELPED ME WITH IT.

WHOA, YOU'VE BEEN BUSY.

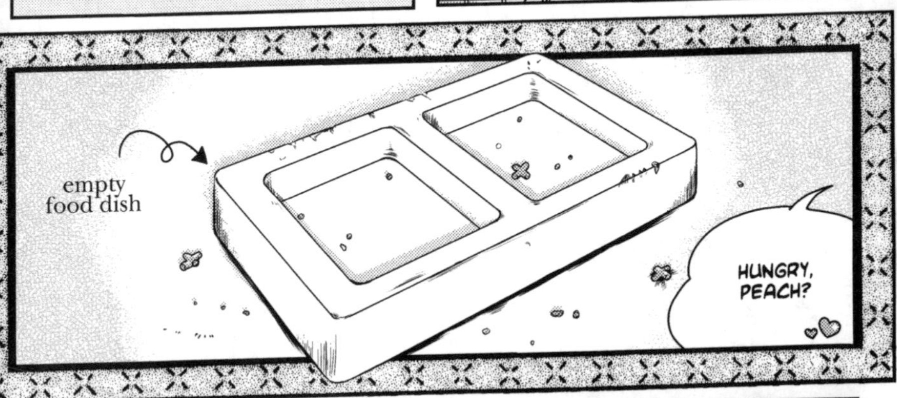
empty food dish
HUNGRY, PEACH?

"FUZZY FARM FEED" COMING RIGHT UP!

click

gleam
fwoosh

CHOMP

AHHHHH
GRROOOD
BASH!
BASH!
BAD!
BAD!
scratch
scratch
click
huff
huff
WHAT'S GOTTEN INTO PEACH?
Rub
slither
NOW HOW AM I GOING TO REFILL HER DISH?

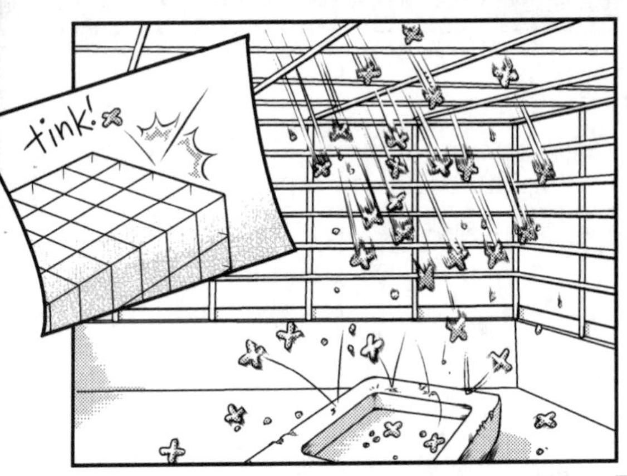
tink!

Doink!

CHOMP
CHOMP
ROAR!
fwoosh

SHE USED TO BE SO GENTLE. WHAT HAPPENED TO HER?

TOK

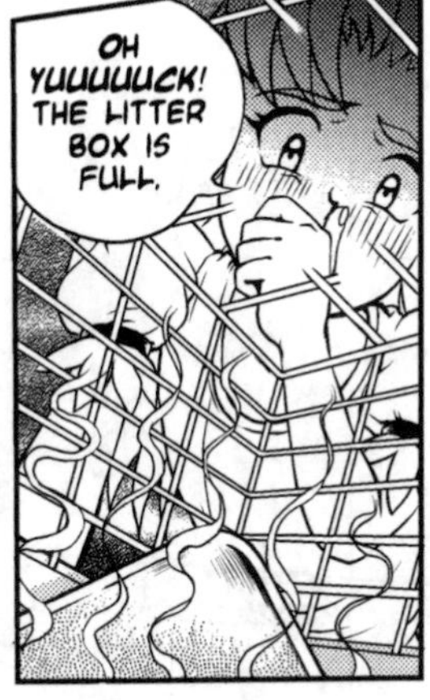
OH YUUUUUCK! THE LITTER BOX IS FULL.

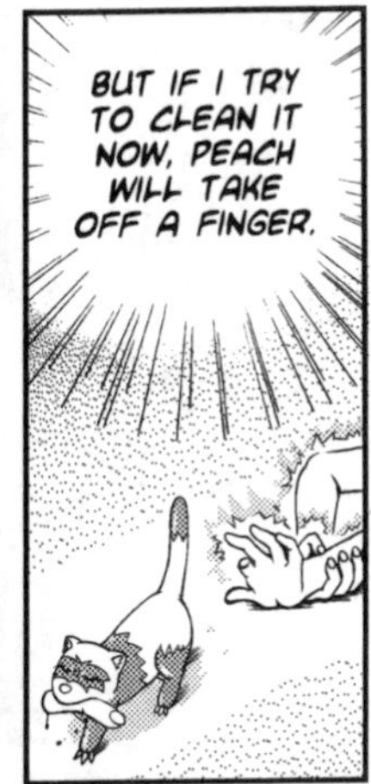
BUT IF I TRY TO CLEAN IT NOW, PEACH WILL TAKE OFF A FINGER.

THE "BITTER BITE" SPRAY!
The bite BITES
I WONDER IF...
Shaaa
SNIFF
EYUCK!!
bleagh
...SHE HAS TO BITE ME?!
WHAT A STUPID PRODUCT.
I HOPE IT WON'T COME TO THAT.
ZZ

NOW WITH
CLUMPING
Cats love it!
KITTY LITTER
creekk
grasp
Tip-Toe
RING
OH, THAT'S PROB-
Hiss!
eeek!
SPRNG
FWOSH
FWOSH
FWOSH
SWOOP
CATAPULT!

Waugh!
SNAP SNAP
SNAP
CHOMP

AAgghhhhhh!!

leggo~ leggo~
SCRUFFING...
TOO LATE FOR THAT!
A SPANK ON THE REAR.
NO. NO!
IF ALL ELSE FAILS, TRY THE NOSE FLICK.
THAT'S THE ONE!

Roll
flick!
MISS

FLICK!
Wick!

GRRR

Ahhhhhhh!
fwump
nip
nip

MOM'S NOT HOME YET. WHAT AM I GONNA DO?
Sniff Sniff
Squeeze

IT'S A BEAUTIFUL DAY AT MUSHROOM MORTGAGE. MEGAN KELL-
MOM!! HELP!!

Click
I WANT TO BE FRIENDS WITH PEACH...
SO I HAVE TO FACE MY FEARS AND SHOW HER SOME DISCIPLINE.
IF I HAVE TO BE BITTEN... SO BE IT.
Shaaa
PEACH?
PEACH...?

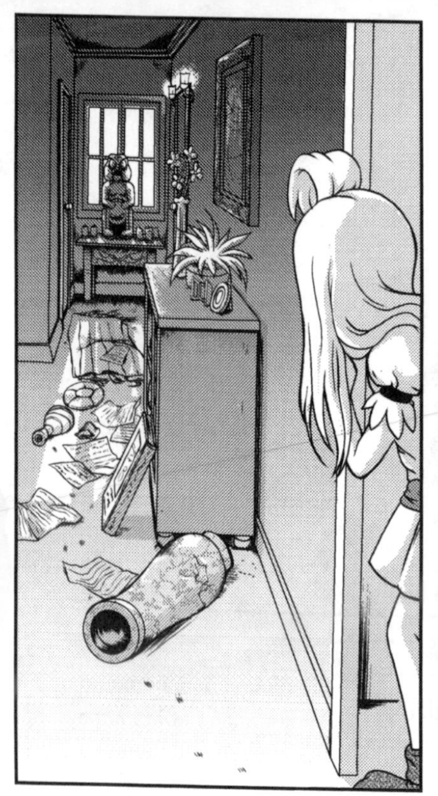

fwump

AUGH! NOT THE HAUNTED ROOM! MOM KEEPS ALL HER EXPENSIVE JUNK IN THERE!

. . .

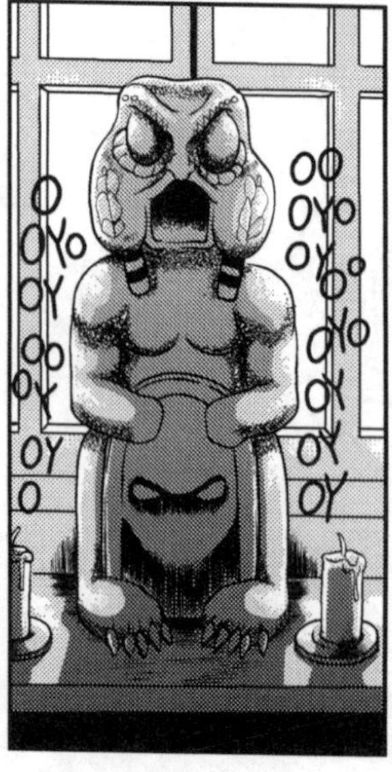
O
OYO
OY
OO
OY
OY
O
OO
OYO
OYO
OYO
OY
OY
OY

Gulp

munch munch
creeak
MOM'S ANTIQUE VICTORIAN DRESS!
MUNCH MUNCH MUNCH

NO, PEACH! MOM WILL KILL US!!
MUNCH

WUMP x2

FACE MY FEARS, FACE MY FEARS, FACE MY FEARS, FACE MY FEARS...
PEACH, PLEASE COME HERE.

LET'S BE FRIENDS...
...PEACH...
why isn't the handra attacking?

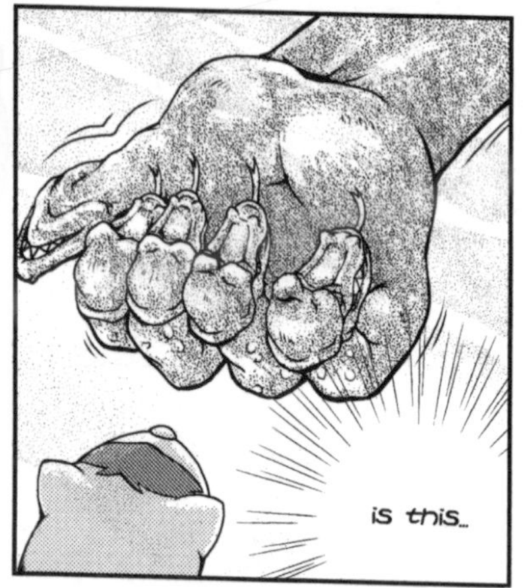
is this..

FSSSH
..some sort of handra war dance?

it's trying to intimidate me! but i won't let it!

this is my treasure!!
i found it first!

i'll make you regret crossing warrior-princess peach!!
Wick!

Sniff snif
strange. the handra's odor is different.

HEH HEH HEH

SWOOSH
ROAR
CHOMP

Wick!
am i poisoned?
RuuuB.
handra! what did you do to me?
it... it has made worms meat of me!
now they rule again. no longer will they fear me.
scruff

BAD FERRET! DON'T BITE!
sniffle

this...

...feels familiar...

it's just like...

mommy-ferret...
don't bite.
princesses don't bite.
Sparkle

DON'T BITE, PEACH.
DON'T BITE.
flop
sniff
snif
handra, i think i understand.

SINCE YOU'RE GOOD NOW, I HAVE SOMETHING FOR YOU.

REMEMBER THIS?
new googly eye
oh, mr. fuzzy! i'm so happy!
i thought i'd never see you again!

Smile

I ALSO HAVE MORE TREATS FOR YOU.
FUZZY FRUITS
Bitter Bite-coated hands

ENJOY!

AND SO, THE HANDRA REDEEMED ITSELF.
RAIN OF TREATS
AMANDA AND PEACH HAD FINALLY BEGUN THEIR JOURNEY TOWARDS DEEPER UNDER-STANDING AND FRIENDSHIP...
the handra tricked me! these treats were poisoned!
i'll NEVER be able to entirely trust it!
...THOUGH PEACH STILL NIPS SOMETIMES.

One of a ferret's favorite activities is sleeping, which they tend to spend about 20 hours a day doing. This is because they require a lot of energy when playing.

As Peach demonstrated in chapter two, ferrets can sometimes sleep so deeply that they can be almost impossible to wake.

A common nickname given to ferrets due to their dominance over the carpet...not to mention a mouthful of sharp teeth.

The act of swimming and zigzagging under a throw rug. May involve a surprise attack in which the ferret leaps out from under the rug at its unsuspecting prey.

Please be careful not to step on any suspicious rug bulges! There could be a ferret underneath!

PEACH'S
MONSTER
COMPENDIUM

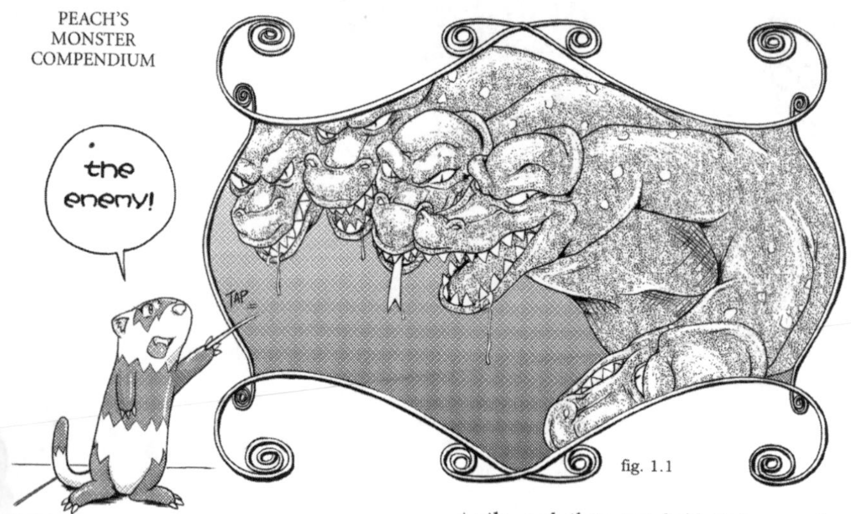


fig. 1.1

# Handra

As young kits, we are taught by our mommy-ferrets about the terrifying monster of ferret lore: the Handra! We are warned that this five-headed reptilian beast snatches up bad ferrets and takes them away, never to be seen again. My littermates and I didn't really believe in them, but all the same, we strived to be good little ferrets...just in case. But the truth is the Handra is more than just a mythological beast-it is real! And it snatches up all ferrets, good or bad!

Having been captured by the creature personally, I speak from experience when I say the Handras are cruel, controlling, unfriendly, and selfish! They seem to take great pleasure in keeping a large stable of prisoners under their control, then pitting these captives against each other in battle. They watch from the sidelines and reward the winner with treats.

Handras also seem to enjoy taking on these prisoners in one-on-one combat. I myself have been forced to fight them on numerous occasions. Handras are very strong! They can use their massive frame to push and prod. Worse, they have a powerful bite with sharp teeth, and they can hold their prey by coiling their multiple heads into a constricting grip. Their defense, however, is surprisingly weak. Their thin, furless hide offers little protection from a ferret's bite and they are quick to retreat if attacked head-on.

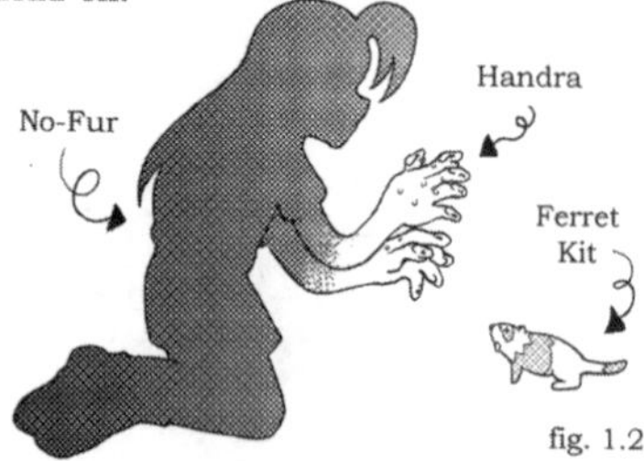


fig. 1.2

It was originally believed that Handras were an independent and free roaming entity. However, we have recently discovered that the Handras are in fact part of a much larger monster: the No-Fur! To date, very little is known about the No-Fur, but we are undergoing studies to learn more. I personally believe that the key to defending against the Handra will come from a deeper understanding of the No-Fur.